GOLD CLIFF HOUSE

WINDY HILL

SILVER CLIFF

SANDCASTLE BAY

N
W   E
S

GOLD CLIFF

SILVER CREEK

SANDSTONE ROAD

To SANDPIPER ISLAND

PINE NEEDLE WOOD

THE TREE HOUSE

THE SAND PIT

FISHING BOAT ROW

THE RABBITS' HOUSE

SILVER CORNER

SILVER CREEK MOUTH

SANDY EDGE CLIFF

THE HEDGEHOGS' HOUSE

THE ELEPHANTS' HOUSE

SANDBANK LANE

Sand Pit Steps

THE ZEBRAS' HOUSE

SILVER STREET

SEA GULL ROCKS

LAPPING WATER BEACH

THE VILLAGE OF
SANDY EDGE

LAPPING WATER LAKE

For Rachel and Helen

With special thanks to
Lucy, Helen, David, Amelia, and Liz

Copyright © 1995 by Penny Dale

First U.S. edition 1995

Library of Congress Cataloging-in-Publication Data

Dale, Penny.
Daisy Rabbit's tree house / Penny Dale.—1st U.S. ed.
Summary: Whenever she spends the night at a friend's house,
Daisy Rabbit feels sad missing her own home, so the roomy
tree house in her yard provides the perfect solution.
ISBN 1-56402-641-8

[1. Sleepovers—Fiction. 2. Tree houses—Fiction.
3. Rabbits—Fiction. 4. Animals—Fiction.]
I. Title.
PZ7.D1525Dai   1995
[E]—dc20   95-16171

2 4 6 8 10 9 7 5 3 1

Printed in Italy

This book was typeset in Horley OS.

The pictures in this book were done in watercolor.

Candlewick Press
2067 Massachusetts Avenue
Cambridge, Massachusetts 02140

Daisy Rabbit's
TREE HOUSE

Penny Dale

CANDLEWICK PRESS
CAMBRIDGE, MASSACHUSETTS

This is the village of Sandy Edge, which lies beside Lapping Water Lake. All sorts of animals live here, so there are all sorts of houses. On summer days you'll find many animals playing down by the water.

Along a lane that winds up from the shore is the Rabbits' green, grassy house. Here are Mr. and Mrs. Rabbit, Daisy Rabbit, and her little brother Digger. They live next door to the Hedgehogs' brown, prickly house.

There is a tree house in the Rabbits' backyard.
Here is Daisy Rabbit getting ready to camp out
in it for the night, with her friends Nelly
Jumbo, Deborah Zebra, and
Nipper Hedgehog. It is their
favorite thing to do.

Not long ago Daisy felt homesick sleeping any-
where but in her own bed. Once she stayed at Nelly

Jumbo's house. At first everything was fine. She

had a yummy supper and a splashy bath in the sink.

But at bedtime she felt a bit sad.
She lay in her jumbo hammock and thought
of her own little bed at home, with all her
pictures around it. She didn't say anything,
but she wished she was there instead.

Another time, Daisy stayed at Deborah Zebra's house. At first she had a wonderful time. They dressed up as fairies, and later they played hide-and-seek under the table.

But at bedtime Daisy felt sad again.

She looked around at Deborah and all the

little Zebras, and it made her think how much

she missed Digger. She didn't say anything,

but she wished she was with him instead.

Then Daisy stayed at Nipper Hedgehog's house. At first she was very happy. But at bedtime

she suddenly missed

her mother so much, she couldn't help crying.

The Hedgehogs were very kind to her.

Mr. Hedgehog gave her a great big prickly

hedgehog hug and Nipper brought her a drink.

Then Mrs. Hedgehog tucked her in gently.

"Sleep well, Daisy," whispered Nipper.

The next day, Daisy felt better, and when she got home, she told her mom everything.

"I don't think I can stay overnight with my friends anymore," she said.

Mrs. Rabbit thought. Then she had an idea.

"What if you all slept in the tree house?" she asked.

"Maybe you wouldn't feel homesick there."

So that's what they did. And Daisy didn't feel homesick a bit. Everyone had supper. Everyone had baths. Then Daisy, Nelly, Deborah, Nipper, and Digger all snuggled up in the tree house. Mrs. Rabbit read them a story.

"Once upon a time," she began . . .

And at the end of the story, Mrs. Rabbit
turned down the lantern and tiptoed gently
away across the backyard.

When she looked back, what did she see?

Five little friends in the soft summer moonlight,
all fast asleep in the tree house.

"Good night," she whispered.